T0065459

TRUE ESSENCE

DANITA STEWART

authorHOUSE®

AuthorHouse™
1663 Liberty Drive
Bloomington, IN 47403
www.authorhouse.com
Phone: 833-262-8899

© 2020 DANITA STEWART. All rights reserved.

No part of this book may be reproduced, stored in a retrieval system, or transmitted by any means without the written permission of the author.

Published by AuthorHouse 09/25/2020

ISBN: 978-1-6655-0213-9 (sc)
ISBN: 978-1-6655-0212-2 (e)

Print information available on the last page.

Any people depicted in stock imagery provided by Getty Images are models, and such images are being used for illustrative purposes only.
Certain stock imagery © Getty Images.

This book is printed on acid-free paper.

Because of the dynamic nature of the Internet, any web addresses or links contained in this book may have changed since publication and may no longer be valid. The views expressed in this work are solely those of the author and do not necessarily reflect the views of the publisher, and the publisher hereby disclaims any responsibility for them.

Scripture quotations marked KJV are from the Holy Bible, King James Version (Authorized Version). First published in 1611. Quoted from the KJV Classic Reference Bible, Copyright © 1983 by The Zondervan Corporation.

Scripture quotations marked NIV are taken from the Holy Bible, New International Version®. NIV®. Copyright © 1973, 1978, 1984 by International Bible Society. Used by permission of Zondervan. All rights reserved. [Biblica]

Scripture quotations marked NLT are taken from the Holy Bible, New Living Translation, copyright © 1996, 2004, 2007. Used by permission of Tyndale House Publishers, Inc. Carol Stream, Illinois 60188. All rights reserved. Website

Scripture quotations marked RSV are taken from the Revised Standard Version of the Bible, copyright © 1946, 1952, 1971 by the Division of Christian Education of the National Council of the Churches of Christ in the USA. Used by permission.

The Mounce Reverse-Interlinear™ New Testament (MOUNCE) Copyright © 2011 by William D. Mounce. Used by permission. All rights reserved worldwide. "Reverse-Interlinear" is a trademark of William D. Mounce.

DESTINED TO WIN

HAVE YOU EVER FELT LIKE LIFE was spiraling out of control? That no matter what you do, you just cannot get it right. It is time to stop thinking like that. If we are destined to win, we must let negative thoughts go. And allow our destiny to manifest in our lives. Ecclesiastes 3:1 KJV state, "To everything there is a season and a time to every purpose under heaven." Which means in our lives we all have seasons we have to overcome. It can either be a blessing or a lesson. There are people/things in our lives that are only meant for a season that we try to hold on to. You cannot force things to happen that was not meant to be.

We must learn how to "let go" of things that hold us back. It may hurt for a time but believe me in the long run it will be well worth it. God does not give us more than we can handle. He loves us unconditionally. Let him in and God will work wonders in your life. God loves us so much; he allows us to make our own decisions good or bad. Even though he already knows what we will do or say. He is there for us, just call his name. God only wants the best for his children. Even when we make mistakes, he will help us through. Trust him, God will never let you down.

When we decide not to listen to the wisdom of God, we block our own blessings. Why do we do that? The fear of the unknown can hold us hostage. We must stop letting fear and doubt cloud our better judgement. Take a leap of faith. When God closes one door, he opens another one better than what we could ever imagine. Too many of us get stuck on the past. We hold onto past hurts, grudges, disappointments, and heartbreak too long. Let it go and let GOD heal your heart. He is the answer to all our troubles. Keep your faith and trust in GOD.

In Genesis, Adam, and Eve disobeyed God, then lost his favor. But he still loved and provided for them. Do not think he would not do the same for us. No matter how many times we may mess up. God loves us unconditionally. Ask for forgiveness and be set free. We are all God's children and he wants the very best for us. There will be times when he needs to break us, so he can show us that all we need is him in our lives. No one said our road would be easy. But having God in our lives during the difficult times makes it easier. God always has our backs. He is awesome.

God will show us what we need to see, even if we decide not to listen. We must make the choice to take ourselves out of that toxic situation. Or we will just keep repeating the same cycle repeatedly. Do you know how much heart break we could avoid if only we listened to our gut more? If we just paid attention to the signs that we choose to ignore. We get too comfortable in our dysfunction. It is time to stop living like that. Let go and let GOD.

Get out of that toxic relationship. You have been living miserable for years because you are afraid of being alone. Leave that job that does not bring you joy. Step out on faith and start that business you always wanted to. God will get you through it. Just believe that you can do it and it will be done. Be bold and courageous. Take heed to all warning signs. And always remember actions speak louder than words.

In the world today, people do not know what respect, loyalty and honesty is. There is no real integrity anymore. Men and woman lie to each other just to get what they want. The word commitment is extinct. Everyone wants variety instead of being with just one person. Relationships/friendships must be based on trust, loyalty, love, and communication to make it work. You should have the same beliefs and morals too. Unequally yoked people cannot succeed in a relationship. It is a real rare occasion if you can find someone that will be honest and love you unconditionally. Men and women both throw the word "love" around like it is a piece of candy. Be upfront with what you want. Communication is key.

With relationships, put God first that will always work out for the best. Treat others the way you would like to be treated. Relationships based on lies or just sex will not work either. It may be fun for a little while, but someone will get hurt. We want things quick; no one has any real patience anymore. Today it is all about social media. You must meet people online, chat on Facebook or Instagram. Can you even remember the days when you met someone at the mall and talked on the phone? Everything must be done through text messaging these days. These are crazy times.

Does anyone even care about romance anymore? It is all about getting satisfied now. Why would men buy the cow if they can get the milk for free? Ladies need to stop just giving it up for free. Friendships are not being taken seriously. It is all about how you can use that person for your benefit. People need to be blessed not used.

God made man to be an image of him, to be a provider and protector. Woman were made to be a man's helpmate not someone to be used, abused, and played with. Some men do not understand that. They would not realize a good woman if they got slapped in the face with her. If we want to live the life God promised us, we must learn how to love one another. It is just that simple.

We must start following god's plan for our lives, it will be for the best. Pray for strength and wisdom. People will come in and out of our lives, the good ones will stay. Some will be for you; most will be against you. But you still must live your life to the fullest. It does not matter what other's think of you, only what God thinks of you. Do not fear. God will never abandon or leave you. He is with us through all obstacles.

Do not let the past hold up your destiny. Do not live with regrets. We have all made mistakes and been hurt. It is how we come through the difficulties, that show us how strong we truly are. Let go of all the negative energy and speak blessings to your life. The power of the tongue can be life or death. So be careful on what you think and speak. Replace bad with good. Wake up every day feeling blessed. Be grateful that you are still here. Remember God is in control.

Our environments can have a huge impact on how we grow up also. If you lived in dysfunction more than likely you will be the same way. You can break the cycle though it is up to you. You do not have to be defeated by the devil. Some stay married to their addictions of sex, alcohol, drugs because that is what they are used too. But you do not have to live like that. Pray about it and get the help needed. You can change.

Matthew 19:26 NIV states, "With God all things are possible." You need God in your life and that is a fact. Live a life you can be proud of. A life that pleases God not people. All have sinned, and we can all be forgiven. Just ask and repent. We are passing up blessings because we feel it is not the right time. What if there is not a right time? Will you give up on your dream? You must step out in faith. Walk in your purpose and fulfill your destiny. Stop holding on to the past. Praise God for the things he has done in your life.

Philippians 4:6 NLT states "Do not worry about anything; instead, pray about everything." Deuteronomy 31:8 RSV states, "It is the Lord, who goes before you, he will be with you, he will not leave you or forsake you. Do not fear or be dismayed. 2 Timothy 1:7 "for God did not give us a spirit of fear, but of power and of love and self-control. John 8:32 NLT "And you will know the truth, and the truth will set you free." God will show us mercy and grace. You are alive for a reason; God does not make mistakes.

Know that your life is worth living. There is someone who needs exactly what you have to offer. Keep negative out, bring positive in. When you know your worth, you will never let another person devalue you. Know who you are in God. "You are worthy." "You are blessed." "You are marvelously and wonderfully made." Be the best version of you.

During the tough times, remember the devil does not win. Do not ignore the signs. No one is worth your integrity. Be honest with yourself and others. Do what you say and say what you mean. Never let someone steal your joy. Push through the roadblocks and get your breakthrough. Increase your faith and watch the blessing start to flow.

Keep God in your life. Do not let others block your blessings. Always remember to stay positive even when it is hard. Do not let fear stop you. Let go and let God work a miracle in your life. Repent and ask forgiveness if necessary. Pray about everything and give thanks daily. In this journey we call life, we will have setbacks, heartbreak, disappointments, and betrayals. Remember this through it all, we are destined to win.

Here are a few scriptures I like to ready daily: Psalm 23, Psalm 27, Proverbs 2, and Ecclesiastes 3:1-8

Thank you and God bless.

THE ADDICT

He was a tall light skin brother who worked at Habitat for Humanity. He was mysterious, never smiled. The females loved him; the guys hated him. He set his sights on a young sexy volunteer. Little did she know, that would be the worst mistake of her life. It was August of 2014; he knew he would have her. His name was Ty.

Ty had everyone fooled, he could bull shit his way through anything. He was dating his best friend Deidre, even though he would not admit it. What he wanted now was the sexy woman that caught his eye. Ty seemed to have a good heart. He helped people if they needed it. He enjoyed cooking. He seemed to be the perfect catch. But as they say looks can be deceiving. And in this case, they were. Ty was a man without a soul. He knew he would never be good enough. So, he had to pretend to be someone he could never be.

Sasha was her name. She only been in Charlotte a few months. Had not met too many people yet and her boyfriend (the love of her life) was in jail. When she met Ty, she thought he was charming and sexy. He invited her over one night. Do you want to come by my place tonight? Ty asked. Yes, what time should I be there? Sasha responded back. They danced to music and talked with his neighbor. He was not so serious like he was at work. They laughed and had a great time. Before the night was over Ty was inside of her in front of the huge mirror in his living room. That was all part of his plan.

Ty and Sasha started hanging out a lot at his place. He did not drive so she would go over there or pick him up from work. She still volunteered at Habit for Humanity a few times a week. As she learned more about him and watched him. She realized he was a pathological liar. (Someone who lies for no apparent reason) Ty had told Sasha that he was not involved with anyone else. She found out differently the night he asked her over and someone else was there. What the hell is going on? You asked me over. Sasha said. I tried to call you with my change of plans. Ty said. Which was complete bullshit. It would be his best friend Deirdre. Sasha went inside anyway and was not leaving. Deirdre finally got the message and took her ass home. Sasha was mad at first, but he was fun to be around, so what the hell. She had not met anyone else yet. And the sex was great between them. She learned that he was originally from Chicago Illinois. He had two brothers and two sisters. They were not a close-knit family at all. His father had died years ago. His mom had all her children by married men. So, right there you can tell commitment and honesty was an issue with this family.

Ty was an ex- marine who was now divorced and had two children that hardly spoke to him. His daughter lived within a half hour distance and hardly tried to see him. He has ruined every relationship he has ever had because of his deceit. And that is something he will do until the day he dies. (Ruin lives) He really thought he had Sasha fooled but little did he know she could see right through his game. She always knew there was something seriously wrong with him. (He was a psychopath) He thought he was God's gift to woman. What he did not know was that his female friends only kept him around for money especially Dierdre. Who was a pathetic older woman who worshiped the ground he walked on.

Ty was a man with nothing to show for his life, bad credit, no car, no license, a mediocre job that he hated. He was also an alcoholic and sex addict. He had no real plans for his life. But he was content, he had Deirdre who came over every Sunday after church. Plus, he had Sasha he would spend every night with after work. He had it good. Ty was a complete loser that pretended to be what you wanted him to be. Deep down he hated himself. He had no respect for woman, his family, or his co-workers. The only good thing you could really say about Ty is that he would give you money if you needed it. He had no real emotion, no feelings at all. He thought life was one big joke. You try to have a serious conversation with him, and he laugh it off. Nothing could affect him. He believed his own lies. If you asked a question the first thing he would do is lie. Sasha saw right through him for who he truly was. Unfortunately, he had others fooled, especially his family. They were not with him daily like she was, they were in Chicago. Sasha had already dealt with someone like him before, so she knew what to look for. Ty never knew how much she really knew about him. He was convinced Sasha believed all his lies and that is exactly what she wanted him and his family to believe. She had them all fooled.

Sasha had Ty so fooled, he started giving her the key to his place. The things you can find out about people. The lies he told other women. The pornos hidden in his drawer. You would not believe it. Ty had to have his two beers after work daily. Weekends were for Vodka or Gin. He really did have some issues. He contradicted himself all the time. He was always saying one thing and doing another. Sasha acted like she thought she should. A little jealous, a little protective. She made him feel like a man that was worthy of her. And it worked. She got what she wanted from him.

On the weekends, they would chill at his place. Or go to the flea market. Sasha knew Deirdre was still coming to see him on Sundays and never said a word. It would not have nattered anyway Ty did not care about her feelings. See this is the type of shit woman deal with when they have low self-esteem and just do not want to be alone. When you are going through a period of deep depression you accept whatever you can get. You just want to feel loved by someone even when you know it is not real. She tried to make sure to never make him mad, because her money supply would be right out the door. Sasha worked two jobs but still if a man was going to be in her life. He had to do his part. And she made sure Ty gave her what she wanted. He is a complete fool when it comes to women. Or he would know the only reason why woman want him in their lives is for money.

A year later, Deirdre started getting mad he was not spending as much time with her anymore. So, Ty started lying to Sasha that he would be with his daughter. "My daughter is coming this weekend, so I won't have time to talk." Ty said. Sasha knew it was complete bullshit. He was laid up in the hotel with Deirdre. Then call Sasha late Sunday night when he returned. He always had to have at least two women in his life. When one made him angry, he could go back to the other. He pretty much told them both the same lies repeatedly. Deirdre was the one who believed him, Sasha knew better. One-night Ty said, “I love you.” Sasha was so shocked she could not even respond and did not.

Six months later, Ty still hated his life. He still drank every night and smoked cigarette; He had a huge porno collection. (DVD” S and books) He thought sex and drinking could help his inner demons stay at bay but no. He had a very miserable life. Sasha tried to bring some joy into it. But when you are dealing with a person like him, there is just so much you could do. She was getting so tired of his lies though. Shortly after, Ty got fired from his job. “I got fired today, they say I stole a bike.” He claimed, he brought the bike and kept it at work in case he ever needed to ride to the store. Ty did not have proof and a co-worker ratted him out. “why would he steal a bike? Sasha wondered. He has four bikes at home. Something was wrong with this picture. She always thought he intentionally got fired because he really wanted out of his job and the only way he would leave is if he got fired. He was drinking more heavily than before. Ty was in a depressive state. Sasha did her best to help him but that would not be enough. Deirdre did not do anything except ask him for money. Ty stayed drunk most days.

“This is not working for me.” Sasha said. “I am leaving Charlotte and going back home.” “You should go back to Chicago” she said. She flew back home a couple weeks before for some interviews. The day she returned Ty was supposed to meet her at the airport. He was not there, and repeat calls to his cell phone were never answered. She had to find her own way home. Sasha stopped by Ty’s place on her way home. He was not there. She was a little worried but chalked it up. Five hours later he rides to her place to apologize. Two weeks later she was gone. That should have been the end of their story it was not.

A week later, they spoke.” I fell off the bed.” Ty said. Sasha thought to herself, “because he was so drunk.” A loser from the very start. “Why did I ever allow him in my life? Sasha asked herself. Ty had told Sasha so many times he loved her and wanted to be with her. So many lies. A man cannot love someone if he does not even know what love is. And a psychopath cannot even love his own children. And until this day, Ty still has no idea what love is. He throws the word around to every female like it is a piece of candy.

A month later, Sasha drove back to Charlotte to see Ty. It was horrible. He looked like a zombie. He had lost weight and was very drunk. He had empty bottles of beer underneath his bathroom and kitchen sinks. He drunk all the wine bottles off the shelf. It was a pathetic sight. Sasha said, "You really need to go back to Chicago." He had recently gotten his final check from Habitat for Humanity. He could not find a job or get unemployment. His life was going nowhere. He is such a loser.

Sasha knew in her heart she should have never spoken to him again. But no, she did not listen. She was depressed and had an exceptionally low opinion of herself. She just wanted someone in her life. Ty also held on to Sasha for his own selfish reasons. They both knew it would never be. Damaged people attract other damage people. By this time, it had been more than two years. Their conversations were fake. He did not say much. And if he did it was a lie anyway. Ty thought he was so secretive, but Sasha knew things she wishes she did not.

December 2016, Sasha flew to Charlotte. She helped Ty move back to Chicago. Deirdre sure did not offer. "Why didn't you ask Deirdre to help you?" Sasha asked. "I didn't want to." He said. He knew her old ass would not have drove that far. It does not matter how great you treat a person; psychopaths cannot appreciate anything. They take everything for granted. One day he would truly regret not having her in his life. Sasha had no trust or respect for Ty. Once they arrived in Chicago, she realized why he stayed away so long. His family was truly dysfunctional.

Ty would be staying with his brother Tony. It was a small one-bedroom apartment. Tony had his girlfriend Vee over there all the time. It was about to be a crazy situation. Tony did not allow Ty to drink in his place." So, you know they were going to butt heads. The funny thing is that they are so much alike. They both use woman and hold on to their exes for dear life. Sasha could not see how it was going to work. But none of Ty's other family even offered to take him in. A couple days later Sasha was gone.

Ty was now in Chicago miserable and depressed. He would not look for a job. He had been spending all his retirement money on smokes and alcohol. He had to pay Tony rent. He sent thousands to Deirdre and her kids. Sasha and Ty spoke daily, neither had a job at this point. "What are you doing? Sasha asked. "I'm sitting on the bench at the park." "Tony gets on my nerves I really think I made a mistake coming here." Ty sounded so pathetic. Sasha tried her best to keep his spirits up, while he sat on his ass all day drinking and looking at porn sites. She was applying for jobs for both. Every time she spoke to him, he sounded more depressed, but he loved Tony's girlfriend Vee. She would give him cigarettes and talk. He had her fooled that he really loved Sasha. He missed out of job opportunities because he would not answer his phone. Sasha did what she could for him.

Once a cheater always a cheater. Ty started going on dating sites. He wanted to meet a younger woman to help lift his spirits up. He still drank and smoked every chance he got. He had to hide the bottles in the basement, but Tony was no fool. Tony's girlfriend stayed over every night too. So, it was the three of them in one small apartment. Not a great situation, but Ty was doing nothing to change it. He spoke bad about Tony all the time to Sasha. He only said good things about the girl friend Vee. Tony and Ty really did not get along, but they made it work somehow.

Ty was unemployed from August 2016- March 2017, he finally got a part-time job at Amazon that Sasha helped him get. He hated it but he did it. That same month she found a job too. A company she had worked for before. Ty was still miserable, and he was completely out of his retirement money. It took him less than six months to waste away thirty thousand dollars. He did not pay off overdue bills. So, who knows where the money went? He is still such a loser.

Deirdre came to visit him in June 2017, Sasha moved there a month later. He sounded so depressed every time they talked. She felt she had to help him because he had always been there for her when she needed. Sasha was going to help him get his shit together, then figure it out from there. In her heart, she knew she would not stay in Chicago. It is a beautiful city but not really for her. Plus, Ty is and always will be a complete liar.

The first week, they had to stay at hotels. The following week they would find an apartment where his brother lived but across from him. Sasha gave Ty the money to move in. The lease would only be in Ty's name. From day one he never made her feel like she belonged there. A complete asshole. Ty still worked at Amazon part-time. Sasha had to find employment. In September, Ty got a job at Ecolab where he still works today. Sasha helped him find that job. He left amazon. She also started a full-time job. Their schedules were similar. So, it did not cause any problems.

Even with the new job, Ty continued to drink heavily; his moods would change at a drop of a hat. He nearly raped Sasha one night, he was so drunk. "I am so sorry" he apologized profusely. Sasha knew Ty would never change. She knew exactly when he met someone else. He would not admit it. "Did you meet someone?" Sasha asked. "You know I only have eyes for you." Ty responded. Complete bullshit as usual. He started going outside to talk on the phone. He started fights for no reason. And even though he took care of everything, she was getting fed up. It was his apartment anyway, she never felt like she belonged. Sasha could no longer take his mood swings, his drinking, and his deceit. It was time for her to go. She did what she came to do; help him get an apartment and better employment. She was done. He already had someone else in the making. That should have been the end of their story.

The day she left, she went to see Tony and Vee to say goodbye. Tony prayed for her and that is something she would never forget. The only thing Ty said to her was "why did you choose a day I had to work." He never once asked her to stay. Sasha knew then he really did have someone else. Even though he claimed he loved her. Sasha knew since 2014 that he would always be a liar. She chose to ignore all the warning signs because she did not want to be alone yet. Sasha drove away. Ty went to work.

Ty and Sasha spoke every day. They would see each other every other weekend when Ty was off. It was a friendship that was based on nothing but sex and lies. One day while Ty was out, he met a light skinned female. They exchanged numbers. Her name was Carol. He found out they were the same age and liked the same things. Kinky sex, alcohol, and smoking. Carol accepted all his bad habits because she was a desperate soul. She even enjoyed anal sex with Ty. They became close. Ty would be texting Sasha, "I want to be with you, I'm going to move to be with you." All the while he is telling Carol he loves her and wants to be with her. Ty was devious, he would text Sasha or call her right before he went to Carol's place in the middle of the night. Then the next morning when he arrived home, he would text Sasha. "I love you.' Or "I miss you.' When he was with Carol and Sasha would call, he would ignore it or text back a smiley face. Ty really thought he had Sasha fooled. "How would she know I was cheating, and we are in different states." He wondered. But what men do not understand is they always make the same mistakes over and over. Sasha was never a dummy like she wanted everyone to believe.

Ty could look you in the eye and lie with a straight face. He really had his family fooled. They believed everything he said. Sasha was not fooled though. The funny thing is Ty was so stupid he would show Sasha on his phone. He was still texting Deirdre. "hey Sexy, I miss you." He would never admit it though. "Real Men" own up to their mistakes/ responsibilities. He has and will never do that. All his relationships will fail because they are based on lies.

In July 2018, Deirdre came to visit and met his girl Carol. Ty was still talking to Sasha at the time. A month later Ty met Sasha in Ft. Wayne. They had a great time. He was still telling his lies that he loved her and was going to move to be with her. Ty was really a man without a soul. They saw each other once a month, while he was going to Carol's every chance he got. Ty wanted someone to treat him like a man. If only Carol knew of all his deceit. She would not have anything to do with him. He is telling Carol he loves her while spending weekends with Sasha.

In September, Ty's daughter moves in with him. He never knew why. His daughter lies to him all the time anyway so what difference would it make. She is her father's child. She got a chance to meet his new girl Carol. But every time Sasha came into town to see him, he made her leave. He did not want her saying anything about Carol. Children follow what parents do. She sees him lie all the time, so she does the same exact thing. Ty followed his mother and father by being a cheater and not respecting women. His daughter followed him by lying even though she puts the truth on Facebook. It is a good thing Ty never had Facebook. He would be shocked. This is an extremely sick family.

Ty and Carol got closer. In March, Sasha came to see Ty for a week, He snuck out the first night to go see Carol. Sasha found that out later. Ty showed Sasha a picture on his phone and the text came in from Carol. "I miss you." Ty and Sasha had sex the whole week she was there. He really pretended like he missed Sasha so much. They had a great visit.

The next month Ty came to visit Sasha. He was telling her he was going to move so they could be together and all this other crap. Sasha knew he was never going to leave Chicago it was in his blood plus he had Carol. A woman who made him feel like a king even though he is just a boy. When his co-worker gets him fired, he better hopes Carol lets him move in with her.

In May, Sasha went to see Ty. Little did she know that she would wind up pregnant. It should not have even been able to happen. She was on birth control. But it did. She knew Ty was coming to see her Father's Day weekend. She planned a real romantic weekend for them. The hotel was booked, plans were made. Sasha knew in her heart that Ty was with someone else. She got her proof too. By helping him with his Uber account. It showed exactly where he went every night he was not working. And when she asked about it." Who lives at....? He says, "that's my friend Kevin's place". Bullshit no man is going to another man's house in the middle of the night. What is done in the dark will always be brought to light. If only Ty knew Sasha the way she knew him. He would not have come that Father's Day weekend. He would be the perfect pansy for the story she was writing.

Sasha tried to tell Ty she was pregnant by texting him "How would you feel about being a daddy" He would respond four hours later after being with Carol. "I wouldn't like it" That was rejection. So, she played it off like she was joking. Inside she was steaming with anger. Father's Day weekend came. Ty flew in to see her. Sasha acted so excited to see him. Honestly, she could not stand the sight of him anymore. The hatred she felt was strong. He did not want the baby and he was still cheating. "Do you love her? Sasha asked. Ty said, "Don't start that again. I am not a cheater." She thought, "whatever." She knew what she was going to do later. After going to the Zoo and getting something to eat. They checked into the hotel room. As Ty took his shower. Sasha got the baby oil, the handcuffs etc., and slipped on her nightie. This would be the last day she ever saw Ty.

Once out the shower, she gave him a full body massage then got on top of him and rode him until they came together. Ty turned over and fell asleep. Sasha watched him for about five to ten minutes with anger in her eyes. Then she grabbed her bag and left a note that said. "I will not be second choice anymore. Checkout is at 11:00." She got in her car and drove away. Sasha was not sure she would have the guts to do it, but hatred can cause you to do things you would never normally do. She should have thrown away his phone, but she wanted him to be able to call someone for help. She would have to get an abortion. There was no way in hell she would ever have his baby. Sasha and Ty never spoke again.

EPILOGUE

A year later:

Carol got fed up with Ty. She shot him twice in the chest. After finding out he was still with Deirdre. Once a cheater always a cheater. No one came to his funeral. Not even his family, they disowned him six months before. Carol went to jail. Deirdre never married; she died a bitter old woman. Tony and Vee are still together.

Sasha got married to a wonderful man of GOD. They enjoy life.

I have included signs of a psychopath:

1. Superficial charm and glibness
2. Inflated sense of self-worth
3. Constant need for stimulation
4. Lying pathologically
5. Conning others; being manipulative
6. Lack of remorse or guilt
7. Shallow emotions
8. Callousness; lack of empathy
9. Using others (a parasitic lifestyle)
10. Poor control over behavior
11. Promiscuous sexual behavior
12. Behavioral problems early in life
13. Lack of realistic, long-term goals
14. Being impulsive
15. Being irresponsible
16. Blaming others and refusing to accept responsibility

17. Having several marital relationships
18. Delinquency when young
19. Revocation of conditional release
20. Criminal acts in several realms (criminal versatility)

Psychopaths may not always have all these symptoms but most of them.

They are unable to love anyone even their own children.

Also, will include five indicators of an Evil & Wicked Heart:

1. Evil hearts are experts at creating confusion & contention. (twisting facts-misleading-withhold info-avoid responsibility-lie)
2. Evil hearts are experts at fooling others with their smooth speech and flattering words.
3. Evil hearts crave and demand control, and their highest authority is their own self-reference
4. Evil hearts play on the sympathies of good-willed people often trumping the grace card. (no empathy for pain caused)
5. Evil hearts have no conscience, no remorse (they do not struggle against sin or evil, they delight in it.)

THE COME UP

Shante' is a twenty-five-year-old single mother of twins. A boy Nathan and a girl Stephanie. They are five years old. Shante' has had a hard time since her fiancé Lamont was murdered a month after the twins were born. Lamont was a drug dealer who was shot by a crooked cop. She had no one she could count on. Her parents disowned her years ago. Shante' grew up in poverty, a ghetto in Cleveland, Ohio. Her parents did the best they could for their children. Both her mom and dad worked two jobs to keep food on the table and a roof over their heads. Though it was never quite enough, they got by with what they had. Shante' being the youngest was always ignored.

All through school, Shante' got straight A's. That was her way of trying to get noticed by her family. The only people who noticed were here classmates. You are such a nerd? They would say. Why are you such a goody two shoes? Another classmate would ask. Her parents could care less what she did. Shante' was very book smart but not street smart. This would be her downfall.

A sophomore at Columbus State University, is where she met the love of her life Lamont. She was nineteen, he was twenty-two. She was dining with a friend when he came up to the table. "Hello, Beautiful. Can I get your name? I'm Lamont." He asked. She answered, "Shante'" as she looked him up and down. He was dark skin and baldheaded. Just the way she liked. They started a small conversation and decided to exchange numbers. Lamont was graduating that year.

Three months later, they decided to have sex for the first time. The condom broke and Shante's got pregnant. "OMG" what am I going to do? She said. “How do I tell Lamont? Later that evening, while out with Lamont. Shante’ blurted out “I’m pregnant”. He looked at her with a smile on his face. “Now I can leave behind my legacy” he said. She knew this would change their lives forever, but she was not going to get an abortion. Lamont would be there for her or so she thought. His drastic end was not what they planned.

By the time Shante’ turned 20, she had her twins. Lamont was dead. What was she going to do? She could not call her parents. She was still in school. “I can’t believe this is happening to me. She said. Shante’ was going to figure out a way to take care of her kids and go to school. She was determined to not be a statistic and drop out. She applied for paid internships with major companies. She was getting her Bachelor’s in the Management field.

A month later, she got hired by JP Morgan & Chase. Day care was provided for their employees. She would work, go to school, and take care of her kids. Things were still tight though she could only work part-time. “How will I make enough money?” She thought. Shante’ had to find a place to live for her and her kids. On the way home one night, she stopped in a convenience store and played the lottery. It would be a 4-million-dollar jackpot. She thought why not. Shante’s picked numbers that were important to her and forgot all about it.

A week later, she found her tickets and realized she was the winner. “OMG, I just won 4 million dollars. GOD, has truly blessed me.” Shante said. She was so excited. This would help her in so many ways. Shante’ was excited. Once she got the money, she paid off some bills and put the rest up for a rainy day. She did not have to worry anymore. Shante’ was still working part time and only had a year left of school. She knew exactly what she wanted to do when she graduated. Shante’s wanted to relocate to a warmer city. In her spare time, she would look up different cities. It was just her and the kids so she could pretty much go wherever she wanted.

After graduation, she told JP Morgan & Chase she wanted to relocate to their branch in Florida. She was tired of these mid-west winters. They took care of everything for her, paid for her move, found her a furnished apartment and a school for her kids which they paid the first year. The company wanted her to have a smooth transition. Shante’ was appreciative. She still had her winnings plus a great company she worked for.

When school ended for the kids, Shante', Nathan and Stephanie made the move to Orlando Florida. It was an awesome experience. Shante' went from a life of lack to a life of overflow. She was happy. Once there, she realized everything was within a 5-block radius. Even though JP Morgan & Chase provided her a car, she could walk on nice days. Shante' was going to be the new Branch Manager. She felt excited for her new opportunity. God was looking out for her in a big way. She was grateful that throughout her ordeals, she always kept her faith extraordinarily strong in God. He will always make a way out of no way.

Shante's bills were paid up a year in advance. All she had to do was go to work each day and take good care of her kids. They moved during the summer, so the weather in Orlando was great. It rained a lot but not all day. Nathan and Stephanie would start first grade in September. She found them a day camp to attend while she worked. They loved it and would tell her all about it. Shante' loved her new position and the employees that worked under her. Everyone made her feel right at home from the very beginning. It was a pleasant atmosphere.

September arrived; her kids were going to first grade. Nathan and Stephanie were extremely excited. They had met some of the kids during day camp. And were looking forward to meeting many more. Shante' worked early hours so she could pick her kids up after school. It worked out perfect for them. They loved the new place. It finally felt like a real home. Some where they could stay. The kids had their own rooms. This was better than they could ever imagine. God is always on time.

A year later, Shante' found a house they moved into. It was also the twin's birthday. They went out to celebrate. While out, she would meet her future husband. It was not love at first sight, but it grew into something so beautiful and perfect. His name was Jamal. He watched how she interacted with her kids and had to say something. "Hello, my name is Jamal. I saw you laughing with your kids and noticed your beautiful smile." What is your name? My name is "Shante'" as she finally looked at him. Jamal was a milk chocolate brother with a low cut. "I'm here celebrating with my kids, what do you want?" she asked. Jamal said, "You are the classiest woman I ever seen? "I had to come over and speak." "I would like to get to know you." I did not mean to interrupt you, if interested here is my number give me a call sometime. And he walked away.

Shante' thought to herself, "I shouldn't have been so rude." Then turned back to her children. They finished their meal and left shortly after. Nathan and Stephanie were getting tired. Plus, they had school the next day. Once home, they got ready for bed. Shante' tucked them in and relaxed a bit. She kept going back and forth wondering if she should call Jamal or not. She had not been in a relationship since Lamont died. It had been about six years, now. She decided to take a bath first. Then plan.

Once dried off, she called Jamal. "Hello, this is Shante' are you busy? Jamal answered, No, I was hoping you would call. They talked for over two hours getting to know each other. At the end of the conversation, Jamal asked "Are you free this weekend? I would like to take you out." Shante' said, "Yes, the kids will be at a friend. The decision was made they would meet Friday night for dinner at Bonefish Grill. Shante' was a little nervous.

Jamal would text her during the day, they would talk at night. Friday finally came. Shante's was mentally ready for this first date. After work, she picked up her kids and dropped them off. She made it home to get ready for her date. Shante's wore her favorite black dress and sprayed a little of Victoria Secret "Sexy" on. Then put on her heels and texted Jamal she was on the way. He was there waiting when she arrived. She liked the fact that he came early and not late. "You look sexy in that dress." Jamal said, "Thank you, you don't look bad yourself." Shante' replied.

Jamal ordered a red wine to go with their dinner. He ordered the steak she ordered the grilled Salmon. They enjoyed the meal. Then decided to take a walk on the beach. It was a beautiful 70-degree night. While holding hands, they walked and talked. It was perfect. Jamal thought, "she will be my wife one day." It was getting late and he did not want to keep her out too late. An hour later, they went their separate ways.

Shante's arrived home within 20 minutes and texted Jamal. "I really enjoyed myself." She thought. "Jamal is really a cool guy." Then she thought about her twins and wondered would they like him. The next morning, Jamal called. "Can I take you out to breakfast?" she said sure. "Meet me at First Watch" a new place that just opened. They enjoyed breakfast then she had to go pick up the kids. They promised to speak later.

Jamal called later, "Can I take you and the kids out next weekend?" Shante' said let me think about it and get back to you. She was not quite sure she wanted him in the kid's life just yet. Shante' decided to pray about it. The next day at work, she called Jamal and said "yes." They would talk about where they would go later in the week. After work, she picked up the kids, they cooked dinner together. She prayed, "God is Jamal the guy you want in my life?" I do not want me or the kids to get hurt. She slept on it.

The next day Jamal sent a text, "Just wanted you to know I am thinking of you." She thought that was so sweet. Shante got her answer. She knew he was the one God had for her. That weekend they went bowling with the kids and had such a fun time. The kids loved him which was great. Jamal was so bad it made the kids laugh. Afterwards, they went to play a game of miniature golf which was also fun. Then pizza was how they ended their night. Nathan and Stephanie really got along with Jamal. It was an amazing feeling. Stephanie asked, "when will we see you again Jamal?" He answered, "whenever you want." He really enjoyed being with them.

Later that night, Shante' asked the kids. "What do you think of Jamal?" "Did you have a great time?" The kids answered in unison," I really liked him mom, I think he is great." "That's good" she thought. Jamal was good with the kids. This might be meant to be after all. Then she went to bed after tucking the kids in. She continued to see Jamal.

A year later, Jamal was still in the picture. He had decided it was time to ask for her hand in marriage. Things were great between them and he was ready for that next step. He had to figure out how he was going to do it. Stephanie still loved her job at JP Morgan & Chase. She also earned her master's degree. Her life was progressing quite nicely. She could not believe all her good fortune. She was in love; she had a great career with great kids and she still had her lottery winnings. Shante's never thought she would find love again.

Jamal was trying to wait for the perfect moment but that may never come. One night while he was out with Shante" he just went for it. "Shante, you are the best thing that has ever happened to me. Will you marry me? Shante' screamed, "Yes, I will marry you." They kissed and talked about when they would do it. "I'll tell the kids in the morning." She said. The kids were overjoyed the next morning when they heard. Nathan and Stephanie both asked, "What took Jamal so long to ask?" Shante' just smiled.

The next few months flew by fast, Shante' sold her house and her and the kids moved in with Jamal. They had decided since he had a bigger house it would be best. Jamal and Shante' were getting married the next month at the Court House, they chose not to have anything big. A small ceremony with them and the kids was all they wanted. It would be a beautiful day. It was also going to be the first time they made love. After a small reception with friends, they dropped the kids off. This would be a night they would remember.

Jamal and Shante' arrive at The Westin Hotel. Once in the honeymoon suite they see that it includes a king size heart shaped bed, a jacuzzi bathtub and a beautiful very of the city. The hotel staff left a chilled bottle of champagne in the ice bucket on the nightstand and rose petals on the bed. Jamal had also brough a small cd player. He turns on some soothing music. As Shante' walks to and puts her arms around him. They start to slow dance to the music as Jamal whispers sweet nothings in her ear. His penis is erect, as he kisses her passionately. Shante' slides her hand to his penis and gently squeezes. She has been waiting for this night. Her nipples are hard as rocks. Jamal is kissing her sweet spot on her neck. Swaying softly to the music. The heat is coming off their bodies like they are about to set the room on fire.

Shante's kisses Jamal as she slithers down his body to kneel in front of him and unzips his pants. She urgently puts his penis in her mouth and starts to lick it up and down and all around. Jamal cries out, "Damn, baby that feels so good." It is getting so good; it makes him weak in the knees, but she does not let him go. Just as it seems as if he is ready to explode, Shante' stops and says, "No, baby not just yet." Jamal takes her hand and leads her to the bed. She lays on her back as he lifts her dress up. He opens her legs and kisses down her body to her clit. Jamal slides his tongue inside her sweetness. It tastes just like honey. Shante' yells, "Jamal, what are you doing to me? As her legs begin to shake, she has not felt like this in such a long time. Her body feels as if she is about to explode. As she wraps her legs around his head, the climax comes out so powerful her whole-body rocks. "Oh my God, oh my God" is all she had time to say. Jamal is sucking the juices out. He continues to lick until she climaxes again. "This is how wet I wanted her to be." He thinks.

Jamal is ready to be inside of her. He works his way up her body and slides his penis inside. Her pussy is so wet, so tight he almost loses it right then. He gets under control and starts to move in a rhythm to her body. It is as if their bodies were made for each other. He thrusts inside her deeply as he pulls her hair. The deeper the better. Shante's wraps her legs around his body as she pulls him closer. She wants to feel every inch of him. His thickness is lovely. It is like heaven. She cannot get enough as she climaxes again. Three orgasms and the night is not over yet. Jamal screamed, "I love how wet your pussy gets. Now turn over."

Shante' got on her knees as he took her from behind. Doggystyle was his favorite position. He went wild, pulling her hair, squeezing her breast, his penis got harder and harder. He finally could not take it anymore. As he climaxed, he cried out "oh, damn, baby that was good." Jamal rolled off her and held Shante" in his arms. "I am so glad we decided to wait." They fell off to sleep. About ½ hour later, Jamal wakes up and Shante's is on top of him riding him nice and slow. He grabs her ass as he rocks to her motion. Shante's is doing her thing, swirling her hips in circles, making his penis grow larger inside of her. She whispers in his ear, "I'm about to cum, cum with me daddy." They climax together. This time they fall asleep for about two hours.

When they wake, they decide to have a glass of champagne and soak in the jacuzzi tub. They light the candles surrounding the bath and get in. Sasha is laying against Jamal as they talk about their wedding day. "It was such a better day." She said. "I am lucky to have you in my life." Jamal said. They stayed in the tub until the water got cold. Jamal was ready again. As they stepped out, Shante' was dripping wet, moist like a tropical hurricane. Jamal was harder than mount Everest. He could not wait, he bent her over and took her right there. It lasted maybe five minutes before he climaxed. They went to bed. Shante's fell asleep on Jamal's chest that night. It was such a special day for them.

The next morning, they enjoyed a romantic breakfast for two, pancakes, eggs, toast, and more champagne. They fed each other. Then decided to make love one more time before they had to check out and pick up the kids. The kids loved Jamal and he loved them as if they were his own. Two days later he would adopt them officially. This would be a family that stayed together through thick and thin. Nathan and Stephanie wanted to go to Dave & Buster's, so they went and had a great time. Picked up Chinese for dinner on the way home.

A couple months later, things were back to normal. Jamal & Shante's got up and went to work. The kids were still doing great in school. Everything was good. On the weekends, they would always go out as a family. Shante' still had most of her winnings from the lottery. The money was set up in an account for the children when they reached 18. She wanted to make sure they would have money for college. She still loved her job at JP Morgan & Chase. All her employees were still there. She had a man she loved dearly and her children.

5 years later, the kids are about to be 10. Jamal and Shante' are planning a surprise party for them. It was going to be amazing. It included all their favorite things. When the day came Nathan and Stephanie did not have a clue. But they had a blast it was one of the best days of their lives. Jamal and Shante's were still madly in love nothing could go wrong. "I would have never imagined my life to be so blessed." Shante' said. "Especially not the way I grew up." She kept her faith in GOD strong. And that is how she lived her life.

EPILOGUE

Jamal and Shante' stayed together. Nathan and Stephanie both got scholarships for college. They worked their way up to a master's degree. They opened a non-profit to help children and adults succeed in life. Nathan got married at the age of 30 to a beautiful woman. Jamal and Shante's loved her. Stephanie chose not to get married but still had a very fulfilling life. They were all truly blessed to have one another.

AUTHOR NOTES

I wrote this book to show you that even if you grow up with nothing. You can make something out of your life. With determination, faith, and the right people you can accomplish anything. Keep your faith strong in GOD, remove the wrong people out of your life. Accept responsibility for your actions. Stay positive, allow blessings to come to you. Never give up on your dreams. And PRAY daily.

LOVE YOU TO PIECES

IT BEGAN WITH A LOOK. I knew my life would forever be changed. I had to have him. He was going to be mine. This sexy tall brown skinned brother. His skin looked smooth like Carmel. And when he took off his shirt. All I could say is "Hot Damn." The six pack on his body made me want to reach out and touch him.

Then he spoke; my name is Isaiah. He had a deep voice that could make your panties wet. He had light brown eyes that could look right through to your soul. Isaiah's lips were thick and full; very kissable. The type of man every woman wanted, and every guy was envious of.

As I sat there staring at this hunk. My mind began to wander. How would it feel if he were inside me? I looked at the bulge in his pants. I could see he had a nice package. My vagina started to pulsate just thinking about him kissing all over my body. And just as I climaxed, my alarm clock went off.

Disappointment came when I realized it was all a dream. My name is Athena. I have been celibate for the last three years. I got tired of dealing with the bull shit from men. I decided to just focus on me. I am forty year's old with a master's degree in Computer Technology. I have no children. A three bedroom two-and-a-half-bathroom house. I just paid off. I drive a red BMW.

An amazing catch for any guy who is worthy of my time. That dream showed me just how much I missed having a man in my life. I was ready to meet someone. I want to feel passion again with a man. I am 5'5 so he definitely needs to be taller than me. He must have his own place, a good job, be a man of God and know how to hold a good conversation. He must be honest and trustworthy. A man that likes to travel, go out on dates, or just stay home and watch a good movie. I need a man that can make my body shake. He must be willing to go down on me. A good head game is always a blessing. A man that would allow me to wrap my legs around his head so he can lick the clit. Let my orgasm flow right into his mouth. Just thinking about it, makes me horny. What should I do? My vibrator will have to satisfy me for now. The orgasm comes fast and hard.

Now it is time to get ready for work. A new week has begun. I am meeting with the CEO of a company I want to acquire. I could not believe it when he introduced himself. Isaiah is his name. My mind went back to my dream. Is he the man that was shown to me? Would he be able to satisfy me? "Good Morning Isaiah. I am Athena. Would you like coffee before we get down to business?" Isaiah said "yes." He looked at Athena and thought she is the most beautiful woman I have ever seen. I would like to get to know her. She was light skinned just like he wanted his woman. Athena looked classy in her navy-blue business suit with matching heels. He wanted her.

They sat and talked for hours after business was concluded. Isaiah agreed to all her terms. The deal would be sealed at the end of the month. He is ready to retire and enjoy life. Isaiah is fifty-five years old with no children. He is a man of God, who lives in a four-bedroom house with 3 bathrooms that is already paid off. He does like to travel. He has never been married. He was engaged before ten years ago but that did not work out. She was not the one for him. Isaiah is a good man who has been praying for his queen. When he saw Athena, he thought she could be the one.

Isaiah and Athena tried to get together as much as they could. After work, they would meet for walks. The connection between them was felt the very first day they met. It would change both of their lives forever. About two to three weeks later they had their first kiss in the park. Athena asked, "Do you want to kiss me?" Isaiah said, "Yes" She leaned over and kissed him. It was a dry kiss not exactly what she wanted.

The next day he had to go away for work. He would return that Friday. Isaiah made sure he called Athena each day he was away. Athena was going out of town for the weekend. So, they would not be able to get together again until Sunday night. They met up at a park and spent a few hours together. After parting ways, Athena called Isaiah to let him know she made it home safely. Isaiah asked, "Would you like to come over?" They both had to work the next day, but she said "yes." Athena drove there thinking the whole time, "I hope he doesn't think this is a booty call." Isaiah was a complete gentleman; knowing he wanted to fuck her. They watched television, then cuddled on the bed. It was a great night.

The next night she went back over. This would be the first night for sex. They watched television for a bit. Then got on the bed. Athena asked, "Do you want to have sex?" Isaiah answered, "whenever you are ready." Athena asked, "What if I told you I was ready now?" He said, "Come on." Then there was a bit of a hesitation. Athena climbed on top of Isaiah. He was so quiet; she was not sure he was enjoying it. Just as she was about to stop, Isaiah decided to take control. Athena laid on her back, he slid his penis inside and went to work. The bed made so much noise, it was distracting. Athena felt good but could not get into it. The noise kept her unfocused, all she wanted was for Isaiah to hurry up and cum. He took his time. When he finally climaxed, she felt relief. She could not stand the noise any longer.

Athena pretty much stayed over every night that week except for one. They would not have sex again until a week later. This time it was so much better even though it was on a twin bed. Athena had not fucked on a bed this small since she was in her twenty's. It was not what she was expecting. At least the bed was not noisy. This way they could concentrate on each other. You would not expect a bachelor to have such a small bed. But then again, his room was not that big. Obviously, with his other girlfriends he would go over there, or they would get a hotel room. It wound up being an awesome night. It was as if their bodies were made for each other. When Isaiah climaxed, they both felt good. Athena loved to feel his cum inside of her.

They started seeing each other a lot after that. Once Isaiah was finished with his day, Athena would come over. It did not matter how late it was. They enjoyed laying together even if just to cuddle. About a month and a half later, Isaiah made it official with Athena. She was his woman. He gave her his necklace which she wears every day. It makes her feel special. And that is a great feeling.

Isaiah has completely stopped working. Athena took over his company. He can now focus on his passion which is music. Isaiah makes beats for artists and does parties too. He is determined to become successful. In the end, it will pay off amazingly. He will not have another worry in the world. He has the woman of his dreams by his side. He also earns a nice income doing what he loves. Isaiah created a website that went global. He got orders from all over. It has been a true blessing. Isaiah and Athena could not see each other as much with him focusing on his music. But they made sure to talk every day. Athena wanted more sex but that would not happen. Isaiah booked too many commitments. In the long run, he was doing this so Athena and him could live the life they wanted and deserved.

Six months together finally surfaced. They went out to eat at Isaiah's favorite restaurant. "PD Chang's" A Chinese restaurant. As they waited for their food. Isaiah took Athena's hand and said: "Babe, I really appreciate how patient you have been with me these last few months. I know it's been hard." Just as he was about to say something else, the waiter came with their food. They enjoyed the meal. And decided to go sit in front of the waterfall outside. Holding hands, enjoying the moment. Isaiah looked Athena in the eye and said, "I love you. I knew I felt this way for a while, but I wanted to wait for the right moment." Athena said, "I love you too." And deep within her heart she knew she would be his forever.

When Athena could, she would go with Isaiah for his out of town shows. She wanted to support him in all ways. And he loved her for that. One night at his show, Athena saw this woman staring at him. As if she wanted to fuck Isaiah. "I have to ask Isaiah about her." Athena thought. She went back to enjoying the show and did not give the woman another thought. After the show, Isaiah wanted her to meet his new artist. As soon as Athena turned around, she realized it was the woman who was hawking at him. Isaiah said, "This is Cookie."

Athena knew she was going to have to keep an eye on her. She trusted Isaiah completely, but she knew how woman could be. And she had a feeling Cookie was going to be a problem. "Hello, Cookie. Did you find Isaiah on his website? Athena asked. Not that she really cared. But this is how Isaiah made his money. So, she had to deal with her. Her premonition was going to be correct. Finally, the show was over. Isaiah and Athena went back to the hotel room. There clothes were off as soon as the door shut. "Let's get in the shower." Athena said. That is exactly what they did. Isaiah told Athena, "Bend over." As he slid his penis inside her as the water rolled down his back. She put her hand on the wall and backed up on the dick. Isaiah was hitting it hard, just the way she liked. It was amazing. The first time they had sex in the shower. The water got cold after ten minutes. They dried off and took it to the bed.

Athena laid on her back. Isaiah started to kiss her body all over. He started from the toes, worked his way up to the middle. He started to lick her as if she was an ice cream cone. Athena opened her legs a little wider. Isaiah got to her spot and licked. "oh, baby, that feels so good. Stay right there." Athena said. Isaiah went to work on that clit until she climaxed. Her orgasm started off slow and then got intense. Athena screamed, "I'm Cumming." As her body began to shake uncontrollably. Damn, she could not move for like five minutes. Isaiah slid his penis inside her as he threw her legs on his shoulder. He was beating the pussy up aggressively. As her breast bounced, he looked in her eyes. She knew he was ready. She lifts a bit more and took all of him inside her. Athena pulled him closer, so he could hit her spot too. It was truly breathtaking as they climaxed together. Then fell fast asleep.

The next day Isaiah had one more show to do. They would fly home later that day. Unfortunately, Cookie had to be there too. Athena gave her the evil eye. Cookie was a good singer, but Athena could tell she was a sneaky little bitch too. She was not going to get Isaiah. He belonged to Athena. The show was finally over. They immediately left.

A month later, Athena noticed something was not quite right. She had been feeling like she was being watched, especially when with Isaiah. "Is anything wrong" she asked Isaiah. Isaiah responded, "No, babe. Why you ask that?" "I've been feeling like we are being watched." Athena said. "I hope it's not Cookie." Isaiah thought to himself. He realized a couple weeks ago he had a stalker. Isaiah did not want to worry Athena, so he never said anything. He knew he would eventually have to come clean. Cookie had been sending him inappropriate texts saying she wanted to fuck him. She would leave her panties in his dressing room. He did not know what he was going to do. Cookie was a problem he had to get rid of. He loved Athena and would do anything to protect her.

Isaiah had to figure out a way he could stop working with Cookie. They had a contract that would not expire for another six months. He was hoping to find a leap hole where he could get out of it. Isaiah tried everything he could think of. He was stuck with Cookie. "Please don't let her ruin my relationship." He thought. Athena had been working longer hours lately. She was getting ready to step down from her company. She had to train her replacement. It is time for her to start enjoying her life more and being with the man she loved. Athena wanted to get into her passion which was writing, baking, and cleaning. Yes, a weird combination but these were the things that gave her pleasure. Isaiah would be supportive of her choice. They always had each other's backs.

Six months go by, Athena is writing her first book. Isaiah is out of his contract with Cookie. Things have gotten worst though. Cookie has turned into a complete stalker. He must do something about it and soon. Cookie is going to take it too far and jeopardize what he has with Athena. Athena had been feeling a distance growing between her and Isaiah. When she asks, "what is going on?" He always says "nothing." She knows he is lying. Isaiah does not understand how well she really knows him. Athena loves him and knows he is a good man. But something is off. She was going to figure out what it was.

One day, Cookie knocked on the door. Athena answered, "What the hell do you want?" "How do you know where we live?" Cookie said, "I am here to see Isaiah." "You have no business being here." Athena said. Cookie tried to force herself inside, Athena punched her and shut the door. Then she called Isaiah, "Why the hell is Cookie looking for you?" "How does she know where we live?" Isaiah was so caught off guard; he did not say a word. Then he said, "I have something to tell you when I get home." When he arrived later, he told Athena everything. How Cookie was stalking him; showing up wherever he performed. I did not want to tell you because I did not want to worry you. I thought I could handle it myself. Athena said, "we promised to tell each other the truth no matter what remember." "You should have told me." We must handle this problem. They figured out what they would do.

A week later, Cookie followed Isaiah to his hotel room. He was doing a show out of town the next day. Athena was already in the room. "Why are you stalking my husband? She asked Cookie. Then she knocked her out. Isaiah carried her to the bathroom and put her in the tub. Athena picked up the saw and got to work. They took turns cutting her up. Afterwards, they put Cookie's body parts into suitcases they already had. Athena bleached down the bathroom. Then they decided to lay down for a few hours until it was dark. Once woke, they drove to the river and dumped Cookie's body. No one would miss her yet because she had been telling everyone she would be gone for a month sabbatical. She placed that announcement on all her social media outlets. Isaiah and Athena had nothing to worry about. They would take this secret to the grave.

A month later, Isaiah surprised Athena with a trip to Hawaii. It was a five-day four-night all-inclusive vacation. They so desperately needed. It has been two years of being together at this point. Isaiah was going to propose to Athena while there. He had it all planned out. It would be the last night they were there. Athena could not wait to go. She was so excited because this would be their first time in Hawaii. They would leave the following week. Athena had already written two books that sold and was working on a third. Isaiah had been doing a lot of shows lately, they needed the vacation to bring them back together.

Isaiah and Athena finally made it. Hawaii was so beautiful. They could not ask for anything better. The water was a clear blue you could see right through to the bottom. Sand warm against your feet, sun shining bright. It was a breathtaking view. Each day they would go sight-seeing. They took lots of pictures. Even tried snorkeling which was lots of fun. The last night Isaiah planned out this would be the night of a very romantic proposal. He did not know why he waited so long.

Athena and Isaiah found a place to eat, they had not tried yet. After enjoying a good meal, Isaiah asked, "Do you want to talk a walk on the beach?" Athena said, "yes." He had on a white linen pants outfit that he got from Perry Ellis. Athena had a sexy red Calvin Klein dress on with her sandals. Walking hand and hand, they strolled down the beach. Isaiah found a spot where they could be alone. He put a blanket down for them to sit. As they sat, he grabbed Athena's hand. "Athena, I knew the moment I laid eyes on you, that I would never let you go. You have been my rock. I could not love any one more than I love you. Would you do me the honor and become my wife? Will you marry me? Athena looked at Isaiah and screamed, "Yes, I will marry you." They sealed it with a kiss.

That night would be one of their most memorable love making experiences. It started on the blanket. They made love right there on the beach. It was beautiful. Then they decided to go back to the room to have more privacy. The things they wanted to do to each other no one needed to see. Once inside, they went straight to the shower first. Washing the sand off each other. Once on the bed, Isaiah went down on Athena until she climaxed. Then she took him into her mouth until he was about to cum and stopped. She laid on her back and pulled Isaiah into her. As she worked her hips and wrapped her legs tightly around Isaiah. Isaiah pounded her as hard as he could until they both screamed. "I'm cummin." They could not do anything else the rest of the night. So, they fell asleep.

The next morning it would be back to reality. Once they made it back home, there was a message on their voicemail. Isaiah's friend Damon had called and said it was an emergency. Isaiah called him back. "What's up? We just got back in town. What is the big emergency? Damon said, "the cops have come around asking about Cookie. Have you seen her lately? Isaiah thought to himself, "Oh, shit." But out loud he said, "No, I haven't heard from or seen her recently." He was going to have to tell Athena. People have finally realized Cookie has not come back. No one has heard from her. Isaiah asked, "What are we going to do?" Athena said, "Nothing, just keep doing what you been doing? She did not want to think about that. They just came back from a great vacation. Even if they had to speak to the cops one day, she did not want to be brought down to negative thoughts.

Athena and Isaiah decided to talk about their wedding instead. When would they do it and where? How many people would they invite? They finally decided it would be September 12th. That was the day Isaiah made it official two years ago. That was six months away. That left them little time to plan. Isaiah had not planned on waiting so long for the proposal. But once Cookie started stalking him, he knew he had not to wait. They had to handle that situation first. He knew she would be his wife six months in their relationship. Isaiah wanted to take his time; he was not one to rush into things.

Athena felt truly blessed to have him in her corner. He is such a good man. She could not have asked God to bring her a better person. He is exactly who she had been praying for. Their connection was real, they could talk about anything. Nothing was going to tear them apart or so they thought.

Wedding day finally arrived, they had twenty-five of their closest family and friends. It was a beautiful sunny fall day. A little chilly but perfect. They recited their own vows as they exchanged their rings. The ceremony was quick and easy. It would be the best day of their lives. At the reception, their first dance was to "The O'Jays- Forever Mine." Then they danced to "John Legend- All of Me" before inviting the guests to get up. They danced all night long.

Athena and Isaiah had decided to wait until spring to take their honeymoon. They were going to Paris, France. Isaiah had a show scheduled three days after their wedding. Athena was going with him this time. It was a good show. She was even able to showcase some of her books. In the spring, they did make it to Paris and had a great time. They stayed for seven days. It was the city of romance.

Two years later, Isaiah had finally stopped doing shows. He would still work on music for fun though. Athena had five of her books make it on the New York Times Best Sellers List. She was feeling great about that. They did not think life could get any better for them. Their life was blessed and very enjoyable. No cares in the world. But it is said when something is going to right a negative will come.

The next day, an ex of Athena's tried to come back into her life. That wound up being the worst day of their lives. Brian found out where she was doing a book signing. As Athena finished and started to leave. Brian yelled out, "Hey Sexy, what's been up with you?" "Have you missed me?" I have missed you. Athena turned around with a pure look of terror on her face. Brian was her abusive ex-boyfriend from eight years ago. Athena said, "Brian, I am happily married. Will you please leave me alone? I have to go" She quickly walked off, got in her car and took off.

Arriving home, she told Isaiah, "Brian got out. He was just at my book signing." "You better be careful; he is very dangerous." A week later, Isaiah and Athena were out eating at their favorite restaurant. They were talking about the future and the places they wanted to go. When out of the corner of her eye, Athena sees Brian walking to their table with a gun in his hand. Briand says, "If I can't have you, no one can." Just as Brian pointed the gun at Isaiah, Athena jumped in front of it. As Isaiah yelled out, "No" Brian shot Athena, who died instantly. Isaiah screamed, as he pushed Brian away and called 911. He would never be the same. He just lost the love of his life. Karma can be a bitch.

A week later, Isaiah held Athena's funeral. That same day he put their house on the market. There was no way he would be able to stay there another day without her. A month later, the house sold, and he moved to Florida. Isaiah was completely retired at this point. There was no more joy in his life. A year later, Isaiah was still single. He had not wanted to date after losing Athena. One night he went to sleep and never woke up. It was said he died of a broken heart.

The End

A MAN OF CHARACTER

WHEN YOU THINK OF THE WORD man, what comes to mind? A man should have strong faith, morals, and integrity. He should also be honest, hard-working and be able to protect & provide. So many times, we think of men as dogs. They like to use woman for their own pleasure. The question we hear often is "where are all the good men at?" There are good men out there, you just need to know where to find them.

Carl is the middle child of five boys. He grew up in a middle-class family. They lived in Dallas, Texas. His parents have been married for forty years. He has always felt like the black sheep of the family. That he did not quite fit in with the rest of them. That would be to his advantage. He was not meant be to like everyone else. God had something more in store for him. His light would shine. Carl was destined for greatness.

Carl idolized his father who was a man of strong faith in GOD. His father ran his own manufacturing company which was successful. His father grew up in poverty and was able to make it. He did not let his circumstances determine his future. He was the first one in his family to attend college. Carl's father was also athletic. He would be the one to shape Carl into the man he is today. His father showed him that through hard work you can achieve anything. He believed in God and made sure his family did too. Carl would make his father proud.

A junior in high schools, Carl was very athletic. He loved all sports. He played on the football team, the basketball team and he even ran track. He was class president and highly intelligent. Carl received straight "A's." Teachers loved him; the students were envious. He could do anything he put his mind too. He stayed focus. Carl received early admission to college with a football scholarship. Instead of doing his senior year the following year. He would be a freshman in college. He could not wait to go to the University of Texas.

Carl would major in computer science. He was always interested in technology. When possible, he volunteered at his dad's company too. That was usually on the school breaks only. He enjoyed working with his father but had no intention of ever having to run the company. His father showed him the ropes anyway. It may be needed in the future. Carl's freshman year of college was great. He exceled in all his classes, so he kept his scholarship. He found a part-time job at the bookstore. He loved books. Carl loved to expand his knowledge and books helped him do that. He even taught himself different languages. Carl could speak Spanish, French, Italian and a little German too. He even knew sign language. He wanted to be diverse. He did whatever he needed to do to become a better man. His father taught him he could do all things through Jesus Christ. And that was his belief.

Carl ran a weekly bible study that most of his classmates attended. He enjoyed teaching about the Lord. He was not into partying like some of the other students. He only wanted to shout for GOD. No one could say a bad thing about Carl. He had a good heart. He stayed positive and loved his life. If you needed anything, you could count on Carl. He was well known and respected from all that met him. He would accomplish all his goals.

The end of freshman year brought some devastating news. His father was dying of cancer. Now here was a man that never smoked a day in his life, a hard worker that provided for his family and never complained. Was active in the community, who was laid up in the bed sick. Who would have thought this would happen to him? But when you time is up, that is it. God knows what he was doing. "Why are you taking my father away from me?" Carl asked. Carl spent every day at his father's bedside. They talked, laughed, joked, and even cried together. It was a sad occasion but also uplifting for them both. They got to say things to each other they may have never gotten the chance to. Carl cherished every moment. He finally heard his father say how proud he was. Which made carl happy.

A month later, his father died. He had two weeks before he had to go back to school. He was prepared for the death, but it was still emotional. He was able to be there for his mom and brothers. The funeral was the following week. It was a nice service. A lot of people showed up to support the family. His father was a well-loved man of GOD. Carl was back at school the next week.

Sophomore year started of sad, but it would be the year that would change his life forever. Carl wrote his first book "Never Give Up Under Any Circumstance: Defeat the Devil." He would also meet his future wife Brandy. Carl still played sports and taught his weekly bible study. It would not be until third semester that he met Brandy. She attended the game he was playing. Brandy was originally from San Diego, California. She received an academic scholarship to attend the University of Texas. Brandy had the beauty and the brains.

Carl and Brandy became the "it" couple on campus. Everyone knew who they were and loved them. They were both exceptional students. Their studies always came first but they found ways to spend time together. Brandy even started to help him with the bible study. They both had strong faith in GOD. They were going to have an amazing future.

Carl was just like his father. A man who worked hard and showed integrity in all that he did. Carl was honest and earned respect. He never gave up on his dreams. He was destined for greatness and would not let anything stop him from getting there. Brandy was majoring in Engineering. So, together their future was bright. Brandy was anything but an original woman. Her mother taught her how to be strong yet feminine. And that she could become whoever she wanted to be. Brandy also exceled in all her classes. She even had a sense of humor. Carl would fall in love with her.

Two years later, Carl graduated and received his Bachelor's in Computer Science. Brandy was so proud of him that she surprised him with a trip to Jamaica. She would graduate the following year. Jamaica would be the first trip that they would ever take together. They were excited. The trip was everything they could wish for. The weather was party, the hotel was great. They slept in separate beds. They had so much fun when it was time to leave, they were sad.

In the fall, Carl started his master's program. And Brandy would start her final year at University of Texas. She did receive her engineering degree. Three years later, Carl had his own non-profit business and had gotten his master's degree. His company helped people that were getting back into the workforce find jobs. He was even working on a second book. His business was successful.

A year later, Carl proposed to Brandy. Currently, they had been together about 7 years now. It was time to make that commitment. School was done for them both. Carl took Brandy to a new "Vegan" restaurant that recently opened. He would do it after the meal. As they drank their champagne, carl looked at Brandy and said, "I love you. Will you marry me?" Brandy said, "Yes." They kissed and left the restaurant.

Carl was ready to take that next step and be the provider like his father had always done. God put him in this position. Now it was time for him to pass his test. Would he pass it? Of course, he would. He had a good woman by his side and God in his life.

A year later, carl and Brandy would be married. They were still both enjoying their success and work. They were a blessed couple. They would take two vacations a year when time allowed for it.

Five years later, they had their first and only child. A girl they would name Tamika. She was precious and spoiled by all. Tamika would grow up to be a fine woman. Who would marry a great man of GOD that had the same qualities as her father?

Thirty years later, carl and Brandy died a week apart. They could not live without the other. They had a very fulfilling life.

THE STRUGGLE OF A TALENTED ARTIST

CJ IS A 47-YEAR-OLD ARTIST. HE loves to make beats/music. He can even rap. Music is his passion. He has been involved with it for over twenty years. The problem is he has not had any real success with it yet. CJ has his own website and sells his beats from time to time but not enough to make a living. He also uses Facebook and Instagram to advertise. He has been in the studio with other artists. But he is still not where he wants to be.

The struggle is real. CJ has been blocking his own blessings all these years. He picked the wrong woman to love. He held on to the past too long. He did not listen. Plus, he is in a living situation he really wants to get out of. CJ is stuck. He fakes being happy and satisfied. True happiness can only come when you have true peace. And that is not something he has now. He goes home every day to a house he owns with a family member he does not like. He locks himself in his room to get a small feeling of freedom.

CJ is a man with a good heart. He would be the perfect for catch for any woman. And his woman Keke sees that. CJ has never been married, he has no kids, and has great credit. His only flaws are that he can be moody and stuck in his ways. He can also be selfish and insensitive at times. That is because he is not happy with himself. Once he is satisfied in his life. He will be able to be happy. He feels like a failure. He has self-doubt, he is stuck in the past and he has a fear of the unknown. Once he is ready to let go and step out on faith. CJ will be remarkably successful. He is incredibly talented, and when he needs to focus, he can shut out the world. Which can be good or bad.

He has been dating Keke about eight months now. He has been trying to sabotage it from the beginning. God answered his prayers and brought him a good woman. A woman who treats him like a king, accepts all his flaws and genuinely cares about him. And he pushes her away. He fears what could be a real love because of his past relationships. They fit together like peanut butter and jelly. But he is scared to give in to love. What he is not realizing, is that God took those other women from him for a reason. They were not the ones who could push him to his destiny. Keke is the one. Hopefully, he will realize before it is too late.

"CJ please wake up; you have to want more out of life." God whispers in his ear. "I brought you someone who can help you. Are you going to throw that away?" Every man deserves a great woman. I gave you one. You should feel blessed. "I should not have to keep telling you the same thing." God says.

CJ will succeed once he gets out of his own way. He battles daily with feelings of not being good enough, of failure. He must stop the negatives thoughts. Keke tries her best to keep him motivated but it is just so much she can do. She can tell him the things he needs to hear but what good is it if he will not listen. The struggle is real. Deep down CJ knows he is better than this. That he deserves so much better than what he has been accepting. Something just keeps holding him back. He can talk the talk but cannot walk the walk. He does not have the confidence yet.

"Babe, I keep telling you, success is in your future." Keke says. It is your time to shine, step out on faith. Stop letting your situation rob you of your dreams. Once CJ learns to believe in himself, things will really start to move. He needs to stop overthinking and doubting too much. He was meant for greatness. CJ also needs to start praying more. His faith in God has declined. He needs to let go of his demons. CJ also needs to realize how stupid it would be to push Keke away. She is one of the main keys that will get him to his destiny.

"God, open my eyes, guide me down the right path." CJ prays. "I do want to be better, and I know I deserve better." "Take away all my negative thoughts. Increase my faith in you Lord." If CJ continues to ask

God for what he wants and to guide him down the right path he will get what he wants.

Keke is going to do what she must, to get him where he is supposed to be. She has already seen the future and how beautiful it can be. CJ has been blind too long, but he will realize just how much she is needed in his life. And how she can help him in ways no other woman was built for. She is part of his destiny. They were meant to build an empire together.

The struggle is real. CJ need to look at the whole picture. Focus on what he wants. And when the times get rough, Keke will be there to cheer him on. To tell him that the talents he has, the world needs. That he was meant to be successful with his beats, arts, and a clothing line in the future. Anything is possible if you just believe in GOD. It is time for him to step up as a man. And do what needs to be done. Success is there for the taking, all he must do is reach for it. If he would stop being stubborn and get out of his own way. He could be utterly amazing.

What is the purpose of having many talents if you will not take it to the next level? It is time for him to go after what he wants. He must have the will and determination to want to succeed. And if he is a smart man, he will keep Keke around. CJ needs to go back to the old school ways. When he was authentic about his music. It made him feel alive when he was making music for fun. In his heart, he knows exactly what to do. It is his head that keeps getting in the way.

"God, I ask that you remove the people that shouldn't be in my life anymore. Bring the right people that will help me." "Take away all negative thoughts and replace them with good." CJ prays. "I really want this Lord, show me what I need to do." Yes, if he continues to pray and ask God for his guidance, he will be guided down the right path. He will be truly blessed with more than his heart desires.

Six months later, CJ moves to San Francisco California. He was able to buy out his family member. He sold his car. And found a nice family to rent out the house that would pay for his apartment in California. He also stayed with Keke. He had let go of the past completely and was able to finally be set free. He remembered "God does not give us the spirit of fear." He landed a great job with a major technology company. The blessing started to flow rapidly once he let go and let God.

A year later, CJ is the healthiest he has ever been. He has become a great success selling his music, art, and clothing line. He left the technology job because he makes enough to live life the way he always wanted. He found a house on the hill that he shares with Keke. He is still in San Francisco where he was meant to be. CJ's faith increased. He is grateful each morning, to wake up and have Keke by his side. She stuck with him through all his ups and downs. They appreciate life to the fullest. They did build their empire. CJ proposed to Keke who said yes. They would be married in the fall.

The moral of this story is that the struggle is real, but it does not have to be. If you keep God in your life you can accomplish anything. You cannot take no for an answer. If you want something bad enough, you will do what you must do to get it. Believe in yourself. Do not ever give up on your dreams. No matter how old you are your destiny can be fulfilled. Pray daily, be grateful, enjoy life.

The struggle is finally over.

THE STALKER

DID HE JUST DO WHAT I think he did? I cannot believe this guy would grab my ass, we just met. He is so damn disrespectful. My name is Tina. I decided to try online dating, who knew my life would be forever changed. His name was Darryl. We had been communicating back and forth for the last three months. He seemed to be such a nice guy, we exchanged numbers two weeks ago. It was all a lie. He lived right outside of the city. Darryl was extremely charming.

Last month, I turned thirty. I was ready to meet a good man. I wanted to find someone I could settle down with. It had been over a year since I dated. It was time to get back in the game. Could Darryl be the one? I wanted to find out. My first mistake was to trust a man I met on a site called Plenty of Fish. That name says it all. I have a college degree, no kids, my own house, and I have never been married. I would be a great catch for any man. I work for a great company. I have been there ten years now. I considered myself to intelligent until that night.

Darryl was the same age as me. We met for dinner one night. We had great conversation, great food, and an incredibly fun time. I felt comfortable around him. I thought he felt the same. When the date ended, I gave him a hug. That is when he grabbed my ass. WTF. I pulled his hand away and played the situation off. We went our separate ways.

A week later, Darryl called. He wanted to meet up that weekend. We chose to meet at a bowling alley. It had been a long week and we just wanted to relax. I decided to give him the benefit of the doubt for grabbing my ass the week before. If I would have listened to head none of this would have happened. Darryl and I had an awesome time bowling.

We played three games. At the end of the night, Darryl aid he would give me a call the next day.

The next day a Sunday, after church I received a call from Darryl. He wanted to take me to lunch. I was hungry so I told him to meet me at the Red Lobster (my favorite place). They have the best biscuits ever. I also enjoy getting the grilled salmon meal. We enjoyed our meal and conversation. Afterwards we went for a long walk. The evening turned out genuinely nice. I really enjoyed spending time with him.

Three months later, Darryl and I were still hanging out. We would see each other about three times a week. I felt like I was falling in love with him. Except for that first night I met him, he has been a complete gentleman. I would find out it was all an act. If I would have paid attention to the warning signs. I would have given up on him much sooner. Friday night we went to a movie. I invited him over to my place afterwards. It had been 90 days, so I was ready for a little fun. I was ready to give up "the cookie". It had been a long time. I showed Darryl to my room.

Darryl was a complete gentleman; he took it nice and slow. He made sure I was very wet before he slid his penis inside. I had never felt such pleasure in my life. It was as if I was having an out of body experience. It was that damn good. You know it is said great sex will make you do some foolish things. He made me orgasm four times that night. It was utterly amazing.

The next day, I called Darryl three different times. He never answered the phone. I was thinking "He got what he wanted now he doesn't want to talk." That made me feel some type of way. I did not hear from Darryl for the next three days. I was getting worried and mad at the same time. "Why would he do this to me?" "What gives him the right?" I thought we hit it off fine. Tina figured something had to be wrong.

The following day, Tina still had not heard from him. She decided to go to his job. "What do you know? He had never worked there. Now she really knew something was going on and she was going to get to the bottom of this. She had some research to do. Once she arrived him, she pulled a background check on the name he gave her. She realized he did not exist five years prior to when they met. "What was going on" "Was he in witness protection?" Her curiosity got the best of her.

"Who was this man I slept with? She wondered. It took a little while, but she finally found where he lived. She could not believe her eyes; he had a wife and two children. Tina was able to follow him one day when she saw him at the store. "How could he do this to me and why?" What was the purpose of him getting to know me? She was not rich. She took a week off from work.

The next day, Tina parked down the street from his house and started to follow him daily. He never even saw her. She was always careful and in disguises. Tina found out that Darryl did not have a real job. He was a drug lord and had many women that he was spending time with. She could not get over this. "How could I have been so blind?" She wanted to feel him inside of her again though and knew she would not ever get the chance.

Darryl stared acting a little paranoid. He thought someone was following him, but he could not be sure. He never even thought it could be Tina. He had played this same game with 7 other woman and never got caught. What you do in the dark will eventually come to light. His wife did not care what he did if he brought home the money.

The whole week Tina followed Darryl. She found out everything she could, where he liked to hang out, who he was with. He would find out that he played the wrong woman Tina became obsessed with Darryl. This would not end well. She went back to work the following week but still watched Darryl ever chance she got after work. That one night of passion turned her whole world upside down.

She watched and waited for the right moment to make her move. Tina was going to get him back for making her feel like a fool. She hatched a plan. If she were ever to move on, she knew she was going to have to kill Darryl. She thought of exactly how she was going to do it. She would catch him while he was out one night. Something had snapped in her and she was not going to be satisfied until he was died. "Why did she let Darryl get to her like this? Tina should have been able to walk away from this, but she had been hurt too many times in the past. She could not let this slide. This was the last straw.

One night she followed Darryl, he came out of a building in a dark alley. This was her chance. She got out the car, just as he started to walk. She knocked him out with the tire iron. She was a small woman but strong. Tina put Darryl in the trunk of her car. She drove to the motel she had already paid for. She got him to the room and toed him up to the chair. When Darryl finally came to, he could have sworn he was in a scene from that movie "It's a thin line between love & hate." He looked up and saw that it was Tina. When he saw the hatred in her eyes, he knew he was in trouble. "Can I charm my way out of this? He wondered. That would not happen. Tina asked. "Why the hell did you treat me like that? "What did I do to you?" I really thought we had a future together. I have been following for a month now, I know all your dirty secrets. You have lied to me the whole time we were together. I could not believe you have a wife and kids. "What is wrong with you? "Does your wife even suspect?" Darryl looked at her and laughed. That was a big mistake. "I've been doing this for years. He said.

Tina was insane. She smacked Darryl across the face. She had brass knuckles on, so it sliced his face a bit. Darryl screamed, "You crazy bitch." Tina knocked his ass over. As he was falling backwards, she stabbed him five times with the knife she had in her hand. Tina then untied the rope and stabbed him one more time. Darryl was dead. "What am I going to do with is body? She had not really thought that far ahead. She had thought to buy a tarp which she laid his body on. I am going to have to wait a couple hours before I can get him from this room.

Two hours later, Tina put Darryl's dead body in her trunk. Tina drove to the next state over and dumped his body. She found an area that looked like it was a drug area. Then she went to an all-night diner she passed on the way. Tina was very hungry now. "Good riddance" she thought as she ate. She drove home having already checked out the motel. The next morning, she got the rental car cleaned inside and out. And dropped it off about an hour later and went home. Tina showed no emotion. She went about her business as if she had not just killed a man. She felt her actions were justified.

Six months later, a body was found. It was Darryl but the police never knew. They assumed it was a drug hit and closed the case immediately. His wife never even wondered what happened to him. Tina was putting money in the door weekly for his family. This was money that Darry had stashed away.

A year later, Tina had completely removed her profile. She chose not to date anymore. She got another promotion from her job. Tina stayed single, sassy, and satisfied.

WHO AM I?

WHO DO YOU THINK I AM? I am not who I claim to be. Who do you need me to be? I can become whoever you want. My new identity began the night my brother took my virginity. It was a horrible experience, my soul died. I would never be the same again. Another spirit took over. I would be forever changed. Playing my role with whoever, I would meet since then. I was gone. Would I ever be able to become the real me again? After my virginity was taken, I realized that was the only thing boys wanted. So, that is what I gave them. Too young to be having sex but the damage was already done.

My brother's best friend Levi was a fine brown skin brother. He was interested so I willingly let him have the cookie. It was a good experience not that I really had much to compare it to. Men are objects that should be willing to please me. If they gave me what I needed. I gave them what they wanted. What I was looking for was a protector. Something I would never get. My brother did not protect me. I had to find it somewhere else.

My first puppy love experience was with a boy Anthony. He was two years older than me. We spent a lot of time together. My parents liked him; his family loved me. I was the innocent girl who made him happy. If only they really saw in our relationship. We would have sex anywhere. It was amazing. Our relationship lasted two years. Then it was time to move on.

After him, there was Floyd, Bernard, and a few others. I cannot even remember their names. It was too many to count. In high school, I dated a guy who had the same birthday as me. His name was Corey. We had the same sexual appetite. The things we would do at school or after school would make you green with envy. There was even a time at his apartment complex where we did it right on the dryer. We lasted about six months. It was only based on sex.

After Corey, there was Lavelle. We were the same height. For a short guy, he had a fat piece of wood and knew just how to use it. We were the "it" couple at school. It had to end when his family chose to move out of the township. I was heartbroken. Due to what my brother did, high school was the worst years of my life. These were the years when my self-esteem was at the lowest. I slept with a knife under my pillow. I thought about committing suicide so many times. I wish I would have done it. I started writing poetry instead. It was deep and it was very depressing. My life was completely out of control. There was nothing I could do to stop my pain. Friends would betray me for no reason at all. I hated my life with a passion. No one really cared about what I was going through. I had two best friends that stuck by me through high school luckily. Even they did not know the real me. Who am I? I am whoever you need me to be.

During my first summer job in high school. I would mean an older man who was white. He became obsessed with me. For a grown man with a little penis, He knew what he was doing. I had an orgasm every single time and the things he did with his tongue you can only imagine. His name was Dave. He was pussy whipped. He gave me money, bought me whatever I wanted. He even let me use his car most days. There was nothing he would not do for me. Until this day nearly thirty years later this fool is still in love with me. But I have never felt the same. I think he is just so pathetic.

In my junior year, I met an older man Robert. He was a light skin brother who wound up taking me to my junior prom. We had sex whenever we could but of course that would not last. He needed variety and we were not meant to be. A woman with no soul cannot ever get what she longs for. A protector, a man who would love her for her mind and not just her body. I am the person my brother made me become. Did anyone know how bad I had gotten? No. Could I have been helped. Who knows what would have happened? Why did God choose me to go through this? None of these questions have ever been answered. I acted like a whore, I loved sex and would open my legs to almost anyone who wanted a piece. But it could not be no ugly dude. I did not care I had a need only a man could satisfy. A personal with no boundaries that had to have sexual satisfaction at all cost. Yes, brother this is who you made me. Who am I? Who can I become? Will the true me ever be able to surface?

In my senior year, I met a guy named Ray. He was a sexy chocolate brother I met at the arcade. He drove a red two door car that made me feel sexy every time I was in it. I was proud to be his woman. He was the first and only man I have ever been with that had a curvy penis. He was my first love. Ray took me to my senior prom. We had a great time too. He would be the first and only man to ever impregnate me. I chose to go to college instead of becoming a mother. Which was the best decision for us. Ray was also the first man I ever lived with. We lasted three years before it was time for us to part ways.

There were others during high school, I was with a guy named Shannon for about six months. When I found out he cheated on me. I had sex with his best friend Anthony who was always interested in me. Some experiences were memorable others was easily forgotten that is why I cannot remember their names to this day. Thank you, brother for who you made me become. Someone I do not even want to look at in the mirror. A person with no morals, no integrity, no self-respect, and no self-worth. A broken woman with extremely low self-esteem. Someone who has been used her whole life. My legs opened to almost any man who wanted to be in between them.

After Ray, I met Antonio at church. A guy that I do not even know why I found him attractive. But something about him made me stay with him for a while and the sex was good. That was the main thing that was important. I was broken and let him use me. He did move to Virginia with me but that would not work out. We lasted about six months, then returned home. Men tell you what they think you want to hear, so I learned to do the same thing. I mirrored whatever they did. Yes, I did not care about the double standard. I acted just like a man would act. My relationships were all about sex never love. What I wished for is if I could have gone back in time and my brother would not have done what he did. I wanted a real relationship, with a good man but that would not be in my future. Who am I? Who do you need me to be? Whoever it is, that is who I will become.

After returning from Virginia, I got a job working for a great company. I met a man; he was a supervisor in a different department. His name was Darryl. We started hanging out a lot after work. We hung at his place mostly, he even let me use his key on days he worked late. I would wait for him to come home. He cooked for me and everything. He was a good man. The set-up was perfect. Who knew I would meet my future husband at the same company? Two months later, I met Dwayne. He was a brown skin brother. From our first date of shooting pool we became inseparable. I thought he could be someone I would love forever. But it was not meant to be. We were doomed from the start. Dwayne and I got married within two months. We took a chance that it would work. It should not have happened. We did not know each other well enough. Our interests were similar, and even our Christian values. But we thought differently about money.

On our wedding day, I knew it was a huge mistake. Dwayne was two hours late. He changed the ring on me. And he did not even show up in his matching outfit to my dress. He sabotaged us from the very beginning. We lived in my parent's basement the first five years of our marriage. This was a ridiculous situation. Everyone thought we were such a perfect couple. Little did they know. I made it last seven and a half years, even though the last year was the most unsatisfying. He was not the man I needed him to be. Dwayne was soft, a people pleaser. He never spoke his mind and I had to be the responsible one. He even put on some additional pounds which made him unattractive to me. I could not take it anymore. I had to get out.

At my new job, I met a man named Kevin. He was everything my husband was not. He became my obsession. Kevin made me feel good, made me feel sexy. I wanted this dark chocolate bald headed brother. I had to have him, and he wanted me too. He knew I was married and did not care. Kevin had a dark secret I would not find out about until three years later. He was a mommy's boy though, still living with his mom. Our story was intense If you need any more details please read my first book "Desires of the Heart" I wrote all about it in my stories.

Each relationship I have had was based on sex. I played a part. And the men believed it all. I could be the jealous girlfriend, I could act like a bitch, I could be a whore, I could even make you feel like you were a king.

It was all a game to win. I have been with two different married men. That was not something I was proud of, but I did not care. I wanted who I wanted. I met another man in church, our relationship was nothing but sex. We never went out on a date. He provided a need and it lasted as long as it could until I moved away. None of these men gave me what I really wanted. They satisfied my sexual desires. That was all they were ever to be to me. Why buy the cow if you could get the milk for free?

I have almost been raped twice before. Luckily, I was able to fight the men off me. One time was when I went to go see a friend in North Carolina. That was right after my high school years. No one knows this real story of my life. This has been between God and I until now. My story will one day help someone. You are probably wondering could I have been saved from a life like this. What would have happened if I were able to talk to a psychiatrist? If I were able to open would I have become a whore. No one really knows. Who am I?

After Kevin, I moved to Georgia. I thought it would be a great opportunity. But like they say you cannot run away from yourself. I had always heard Georgia was the land of opportunity. Was that sadly a mistake? I hated my whole experience there. Even though I would meet a man. His name was Courtney. He was a chocolate brother. So very sexy, he did not have a real job. He hustled for money. I thought I finally found a man that had a sexual appetite like mine. But I got to be a little too much for him too. Courtney and I started hanging out every time I got off work. I even let him move in with me after a while. It was great, he would kill the bugs that flooded my apartment daily and we had amazing sex. We had fell in love or so I thought. Love is not what it really was. It was a sexual attraction that could not be denied. His flaw was, he was a flirt. That bothered me a lot. I got him back one night while we were out. I gave another man my number right in front of his face. If he was going to disrespect me. I would do the same to him.

Courtney was born and raised in Georgia. A southern man with charm but also a thug. He had been in and out of jail many times. Things were never going to change. When my lease was up, and I moved to North Carolina. Courtney decided to move with me. We needed two incomes to afford the apartment. Luckily, he was able to get two jobs even with is record. They did not last long. I was able to find employment directly across the street from where we lived at a daycare. The first month in North Carolina was great.

Then came the day I would drop Courtney off at the bus station. And would wind up not ever seeing him again. He had to go back to Georgia for a court date. We both thought he would be returning home. That would not be the case. They locked him up. He would not be getting released anytime soon. What was I going to do? I had bills to pay was not making much money. I was miserable. He had left me in a tight spot. I had to find another job. He wanted me to help him. Did I really want to stay with a man that could no longer do a damn thing for me? No, I did not but I did the best I could for him. Two months later, I would end the relationship.

Courtney's stuff got packed up and I would drive it to Georgia. I was to drop it off withhis best friend who I fucked twice and felt no guilt about it. Yes, it was a horrible thing to do. But oh well I did not care. I wanted sex. His best friend would never tell, he was married. I am a screwed up. I am a woman who will do whatever she wants. I did not care about the consequences or who I hurt. I was already broken. So, who really cared? I had a few one-night stands after that.

A month later, I was so depressed. I thought about how I would end my life. I started donating clothes and kitchen items. I wrote out a letter to my parents and my best friend. I even had a pile for each person that I was leaving things for. I was completely ready to die. Just as I finished everything I needed to do. I was about to walk out the door when my phone rang. I got a call about a job I really wanted at a bookstore. Even though it would eventually not come through. I was excited about the job and that stopped me from doing what I really wanted to do, kill myself. As you see I am still here.

I worked and I volunteered at a place called Habitat for Humanity. I met a man that first day and I would follow him home. He was originally from New York and designed women clothes. He was a very fascinating man. I enjoyed his company. We had sex. He let me have a few dresses. It was a great arrangement. It lasted two months. Then I met a light skin man named Tyrone. We had an extremely complicated and crazy relationship. I will not get into too many details. Please read my other story called "The Addict" you will know exactly what happened between me and him. This would be a love/hate relationship that would nearly last five years.

January 2018. I would move to Columbus Ohio. I was still dealing with Tyrone for a bit. We saw each other when we could. You are probably wondering why Ohio? Who in their right mind would move there? I chose it because I had family there. I would have never thought my family could be as phony as they were. People from Ohio are the most selfish people you could ever meet. They are only out for themselves. And everyone there had kids, one or more. I made the best of my situation though.

In July 2019, I would meet two men from an online dating site. They were both older than me. William was the first one I would meet. He was a skinny brown skin brother. Our first date we met for ice cream at a place called "Graeter's" we enjoyed great conversation. We started to hang out so we could get to know each other. He had his own real estate business. One night we had sex, it was good. But I felt it was too soon and I told him that. After wards, he chose work instead of trying to see me.

At the end of July, I met Chauncey the night before I was going on vacation. He was light skin like me. We had a connection from the very beginning. We talked all night long. It was as if we knew each other our whole lives. I had never connected to anyone in this way before. He was born and raised in Columbus Ohio. He acted like a real gentleman. We did not want the night to end.

The night after I returned from my trip, Chauncey and I decided to meet for the last day of the Ohio State Fair. He had already bought the tickets. We really had a good time together too. This would be the first night I would realize he was capable of being unbelievably cheap. William was not trying anymore, so I forgot all about him. Chauncey tried of showing me that he really wanted to be with me. We hung out every day after work that week. The following week he had to go out of town for work. I was really shocked when he found a way to call me when his cell phone did not work. He wanted to let me know he had arrived safely. The day he was returning, I was going out of town that weekend. We decided to meet up when I returned home. Chauncey and I had a nice night. Upon arriving home, I gave him a call to let him know of my safe return. He was not ready for the night to be over. Chauncey invited me to his place. I accepted.

This would be the night I found out this grown ass man was living in the smallest room in the house. He was sleeping on a twin bed. Chauncey found nothing wrong with that. We went to the basement that night. I stayed over but nothing happened. I left early in the morning so I could get to work. After work that day, I did go back over to Chauncey's place. Our first sexual encounter would happen that night. We were in the basement on his father's bed. I have never had sex on a bed that made so much noise. I could not get into it like I wanted to. He lasted a long time that night, he wanted to impress me. Our bodies fit together like peanut butter and jelly.

The next day we talked but I did not stay over. The day after that I would stay over every night for like the next three weeks. We would have sex on his twin bed. At least that bed did not make noise. This would be my first sexual experience on a twin bed. It was amazing though. Our bodies just fit. We kept seeing each other. I gave him an ultimatum. He had until the end of September to decide if we were going to take this to the next step. If not, I needed to move on. On September 12, he officially decided to make me his woman. I asked him if he was sure and told him he still had time to think. He reassured me five times I was who he wanted in his life. Chauncey even gave ne the silver necklace off his neck to seal the deal. He lied to my face. That would be the first night I would have an orgasm with him. That was only because I was on top. We saw each other daily, we even got tested together. One night while we were out. I asked, why don't you use condoms? His response was if the woman looks safe, he will not use them unless she asks. I thought that was one of the stupidest things I had ever heard. One day he may die because of that mistake. Thinking looks can tell you if a person has a disease or not.

Our first weekend trip together, we went to Cleveland to see the comedian "Sommore" we had a great time too. I got the tickets, he paid for the hotel. Of course, he would get a cheap one but luckily it was still nice inside. We would have sex the day we were leaving. Chauncey sabotaged a relationship from the very beginning. Even after making me his woman, do you know he never deleted his profile off that site.

He was still corresponding with other women. He was also still in love with an ex. How dare he waste my time like that, but I already knew he was not the man for me. But I made him feel like a king. He genuinely believed like an idiot that I liked him more then he liked me.

Chauncey and I became best friends though. We shared everything but the truth. After his birthday in October, our sex life had a major decline. I knew he started seeing someone else. His excuse was he needed time to miss me, which was complete bullshit. The truth was he wanted to spend some days with someone else. But it was cool. Just like him. There was someone else I could call too. He started showing his true colors. He stopped doing things he would normally do. My feelings did not matter to him at all. It was all about what he wanted. In my head, I was already saying. I would only be here a couple more months anyway. It was never a love connection. It was good sex between two grown people.

My birthday was in November, we went to Niagara Falls. We had a great time. But when I looked at him, I really did not like what I saw anymore. I could not even get birthday sex from him. He pissed me off so bad by the time we got home. I did not even want to sleep with him anymore. The next night after work, I had sex with someone else right before I went to his place. Yes, I took a shower first. I felt no guilt as I lay up under Chauncey that night. He did not want to give me what I wanted anymore so someone else did. He was doing the same damn thing anyway.

We spent Thanksgiving Day together, he spent that night at his brothers and his other woman's. We did not hang out again until the weekend after. There was always some bull shit excuse of why we could not get together. He really thought I was a fool. I tried to warn him that he could not lie to me. I would see right through it, but he did not want to believe, we had sex only when he was in the mood.

Christmas, we also spent together and even cooked. It was a nice day of watching classic movies like "It's a Wonderful Life" and "A Christmas Story". We had sex that day. It was amazing. Chauncey's job was ending the last day of December. He said, he wanted to move to San Fran to be with his mom. I knew that would not happen. He has always been full of talk no action. The type of man that will tell you what he thinks you want to hear. A man that has only lived by himself one time. He said, I could move with him. Which was complete bullshit.

By February, I was out of Ohio. I did get a chance to meet Chauncey's mom in San Francisco. His true colors really showed then. He was a complete ass the whole time I was there. There was no love lost though. I had no more respect for him. Then he had a nerve to try to blame me for his faults. And that is when I went off through text. I told him that he was not even a man. That he was a boy in a man's body and that he needs to grow up. Yes, I put him in his place. He was not going to talk to me that way and have me not respond. Hell, no!

After California, I did have to go back to Ohio to finish some business. He came back the day before I left. I still picked him up from the airport. If nothing else, I am always a woman of my word. We did have sex that night but really that was about me. The breakup sex was amazing too. I knew I would never see him again. Chauncey had always been so full of shit. He said, he loved me, and he wanted me to be proud of him. He did absolutely nothing to show me his words meant anything. Once a liar always a liar.

A month later, I ended our friendship with a "Dear John" letter and returned his necklace too. I had not worn it in over a month. I lost so much respect for him. I did what I was supposed to do for him and made his life better. Now he can make a better life with his new girl Marie. I wish them the best too.

Have you realized throughout my whole life; my relationships have been based on sex only? I have never felt "real love" from anyone except my parents and best friend. Men are liars and always will be in my eyes. They are only necessary for sex and money. I am damaged. I am broken. Will I ever be whole? Brother, why did you have to do this to me? And you hate me. I should hate you, but I do not. My story may help someone else. I cannot trust anyone. My soul is still gone. The reason why I am still here is because my faith never changed. Yes, I believe God is punishing me, but I am not going to let the devil defeat me. I am alive for a reason.

Remember this: God does answer prayers if you ask the right thing. He knew none of those men in my life was worthy of me. That is why he let them walk away. I just did not know. It has taken me a long time to realize, that what is between my legs should not be shared with just anyone. There is a price you pay, each time you let someone in. I do not have to let my past determine my future. I do not have to stay damaged. I can overcome this. My life is worth living whether I believe it or not. "Can a person with no soul change? Can I become a "Proverbs 31" woman? Will I ever fulfill my destiny? Will true love ever find me?

My identity was stolen by my brother. I became who people needed me to be. I was depressed. I was suicidal. I did not know my self-worth. I do not want to live like that anymore. God, please heal me so I can move on and be blessed.

Who am I? Just a nobody that is invisible.

Printed in the United States
By Bookmasters